A Big Surprise

A Big Surprise

Kristi T. Butler
Illustrated by Pamela Paparone

Green Light Readers
Harcourt, Inc.
Orlando   Austin   New York   San Diego   Toronto   London

Here is the dog.

Here is the frog.

Here is the cat.

Here is the hat.

Here is the fox.

Here is the box.

Here is the house.

Here is the mouse.

Here is the snake.

Here is the cake.

What a big surprise!

SURPRISE!

The animals in the story brought gifts to the mouse for her birthday. You can make a gift, and write clues to help a friend or classmate guess what it is.

WHAT YOU'LL NEED

construction paper

markers, colored pencils, or crayons

glitter, glue, ribbons, or anything else you would like to use to decorate your gift

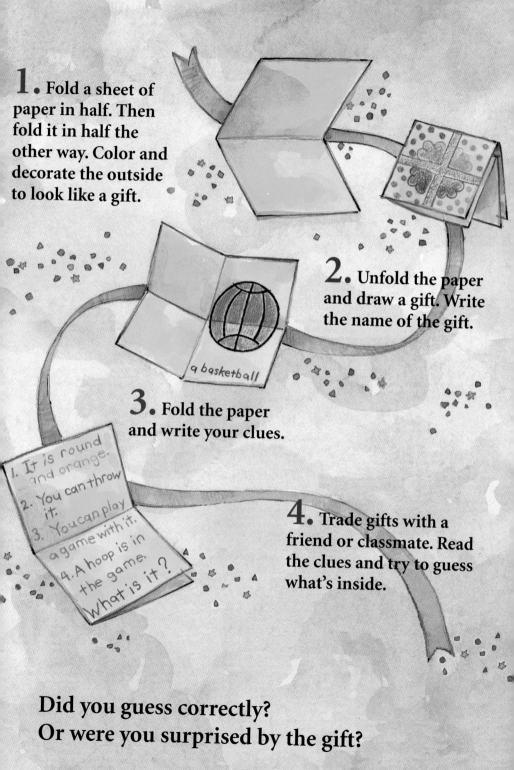

1. Fold a sheet of paper in half. Then fold it in half the other way. Color and decorate the outside to look like a gift.

2. Unfold the paper and draw a gift. Write the name of the gift.

a basketball

3. Fold the paper and write your clues.

1. It is round and orange.
2. You can throw it.
3. You can play a game with it.
4. A hoop is in the game.
What is it?

4. Trade gifts with a friend or classmate. Read the clues and try to guess what's inside.

Did you guess correctly?
Or were you surprised by the gift?

Make a Party Snack

WHAT YOU'LL NEED

pretzels raisins  popcorn nuts

small plastic
bags

measuring
cup

large self-closin
plastic bags

3 cups popcorn

1 cup nuts

2 cups pretzels

2 cups raisins

- Measure each ingredient and pour them into a large plastic bag.

- Close the bag. Shake the bag to mix up your snack.

- Pour or scoop out the snack into small bags.

Now eat your delicious

party snack!

Meet the Illustrator

Pamela Paparone loves to celebrate her birthday. One year she threw herself a birthday party with a big cake and lots of dancing. Pamela thought of that birthday party when she began drawing the pictures for *A Big Surprise*. She wanted to make sure that the mouse's party had all the decorations and goodies she had!

Pam Paparone

www.HarcourtBooks.com

First Green Light Readers edition 2005
Green Light Readers is a trademark of Harcourt, Inc., registered in the United States of America and/or other jurisdictions.

Library of Congress Cataloging-in-Publication Data
Butler, Kristi T.
A big surprise/Kristi T. Butler; illustrated by Pamela Paparone.
p. cm.
"Green Light Readers."
Summary: Mouse is surprised when her friends throw her a birthday party.
[1. Animals—Fiction. 2. Parties—Fiction. 3. Birthdays—Fiction. 4. Stories in rhyme.]
I. Paparone, Pamela, ill. II. Title. III. Series: Green Light reader.
PZ8.3.B9789 2005
[E]—dc22   2004022694
ISBN 0-15-205142-2
ISBN 0-15-205141-4 (pb)

C E G H F D B
C E G H F D (pb)

Ages 4-6
Grades: K-1
Guided Reading Level: B
Reading Recovery Level: 2-3

Green Light Readers
For the reader who's ready to GO!

"A must-have for any family with a beginning reader."—*Boston Sunday Herald*

"You can't go wrong with adding several copies of these terrific books to your beginning-to-read collection."—*School Library Journal*

"A winner for the beginner."—*Booklist*

Five Tips to Help Your Child Become a Great Reader

1. Get involved. Reading aloud to and with your child is just as important as encouraging your child to read independently.

2. Be curious. Ask questions about what your child is reading.

3. Make reading fun. Allow your child to pick books on subjects that interest her or him.

4. Words are everywhere—not just in books. Practice reading signs, packages, and cereal boxes with your child.

5. Set a good example. Make sure your child sees YOU reading.

Why Green Light Readers Is the Best Series for Your New Reader

- Created exclusively for beginning readers by some of the biggest and brightest names in children's books

- Reinforces the reading skills your child is learning in school

- Encourages children to read—and finish—books by themselves

- Offers extra enrichment through fun, age-appropriate activities unique to each story

- Incorporates characteristics of the Reading Recovery program used by educators

- Developed with Harcourt School Publishers and credentialed educational consultants